The Saint with Trin and Omega Station

C. J. Korryn

Published by C. J. Korryn Books 2018

Published by:

C. J. Korryn Books

****

©2018 by C. J. Korryn

****

Visit C. J. Korryn's website for more of his books.

https://www.cjkorryn.com/books

THE SAINT

The Saint stood at the threshold of the city entrance, his dark hair waving in the wind from beneath his full-faced iron helmet. A gold breastplate with a roaring lion in silver covered his chest, while his arms and hands were covered in silver armor. Strapped to his left arm was a large black shield with a sleeping lamb embossed in gold. From his waist hung silver thigh armor that hung to mid-shin, and he wore on his feet silver armor engraved with a dove. Sheathed on his left hip was a sword with a cross engraved on its hilt.

The double gate before him swung outward as a tall, dark-haired man of medium build wearing a long white robe and sandals emerged from the control room to stand before him.

"Remember, they have given you the power—just ask for help. You are His son and He loves you. You have been trained well. Remember your training, brother. We will keep you in our prayers." After speaking, the gate master returned to the control room.

The Saint clutched the pommel of his sword and cautiously passed beyond the entryway of the city and onto the battleground. As he walked along the path, he stared in astonishment at how the terrain had changed since the last time he journeyed this way. He remembered the scenery before him as dreary, rocky, cloudy, foul-smelling, and dead. Now trees soared into the sky, their lush branches shading the path. He walked over to a tree, plucked an apple, and began to eat.

He sat under the tree a few minutes enjoying the delicious fruit. Suddenly, he realized that his head was bare, his long, dark hair blowing freely in the wind. He frantically began searching around the tree. When had he taken his helmet off? He couldn't remember.

How could he allow himself to lose it? He felt vulnerable and exposed.

Something rustled in the bush before him, and he unsheathed his sword. He heard the noise again, followed by a low, evil growl.

Doubt began to fill his mind. He had been entrusted with a great responsibility, and he had lost his helmet! He was entering into battle, and he didn't even have all of his armor. He knew then that he would fail!

Suddenly, he felt an unusual sensation on his head, a sensation he had felt earlier as he sat under the trees. It was then that he noticed his helmet had materialized on his head. He had never taken it off! It had been there all the time! He only noticed it when he needed it.

With a renewed sense of security, he readied himself for battle as the beast beyond the brush let out a terrifying roar and lunged toward him. The Saint barely had time to bring his shield up before him, blocking the creature's attack. The Saint stumbled back but quickly regained his balance as the creature bounced off the massive shield.

The Saint's eyes opened wide as he saw the creature that stood before him: a large, hairless, dog-like creature with menacing claws and a long tail scattered with spikes. The creature's long snout ended with a large spike and another spike shielded each eye. It bared its deadly, pointed teeth.

The Saint tightened his grip on his shield. The dog-like creature leaped at him again and again. The Saint blocked each attack with his shield. The force of the impact each time sending him off balance just a little bit more until he fell to his back, the creature on top of him. The Saint used the beast's own momentum against it and threw the beast overhead. Both scrambled to their feet. The creature jumped for The Saint several more times, but each time was blocked by The Saint's shield. As the dog wearied, The Saint waited for the right time to strike. As the creature charged its prey again, The Saint dropped to a knee, blocked the attack with his shield, and thrust his sword into the dog's heart. The beast howled in pain and tumbled to the ground. The Saint returned to his feet and pulled his sword from the creature's lifeless body. He stood staring a few moments at the evil creature and then continued on his journey.

He traveled for several hours with no opposition, and nightfall began to set in. He was getting tired and decided to find some place to sleep. He walked for a few miles searching along the path for any indication of shelter. Finally, he spotted a dim light through the trees. A few yards later, he came upon a house. When he knocked, a middle-aged, muscular man opened the door wearing a white, lace-up tunic with matching leggings and sandals. His unusually pale hair reflected the firelight, wrapping him in a gentle glow, and he had a countenance that would make the hardest of men feel like a child again.

"Welcome. I've been expecting you," he said as he ushered his visitor inside. The Saint felt instantly that somehow he knew this white-haired man. He wondered how this man could have known he would be coming. The Saint thought to ask him who he was but decided against it, for he felt a strange kinship with the stranger. The Saint entered the dwelling to find it simply furnished with only a large cot next to the fireplace at the far end of the welcoming house.

"You will be safe here until morning. I will be in the next room if you need me," his host explained then left The Saint alone. The Saint unstrapped his armor, dropping it to the floor, as he slumped onto the cot. He quickly fell into a deep and peaceful sleep.

The aroma of freshly baked bread mingled with a hint of rich vegetable stew pulled him from his sleep. He pulled himself upright to find his armor neatly stacked, cleaned, and polished next to a tray of food. He stretched and started to eat.

A few minutes into his meal, he heard what sounded like a riot. He jumped from his cot and rushed to the window. Several soldiers were looting the town just down the path. The Saint scrambled to strap on his armor and weapons praying a quick prayer as he rushed out into the fray. The instant he reached the path, two of the looting soldiers, clad in cheap, weak armor, intercepted him. The Saint drew his sword. The two soldiers stopped a few feet away.

"This doesn't concern you!" yelled one of the soldiers.

"The king of this land claims this town!" exclaimed the other soldier.

"These people are no longer under the captivity of your king," The Saint replied calmly. "By the power given to me from The Keeper of The Great City, I will free these people."

The Saint charged the two soldiers. He swung at the first, spun and dealt a killing blow to the second soldier. The first soldier retaliated with a near fatal attack. Blocking the strike with his own sword, The Saint jabbed a knee into the enemy's side and uppercut the soldier with his shield, forcing the man on his back. The Saint shoved the tip of his blade into the fallen soldier's gut.

It was then that The Saint spotted several more soldiers quickly making their way to the scene, calling on their allies for support. He immediately charged the closest soldier, and as the man closed to sword's length, The Saint dropped and rolled, dodging his attack, and rose back to his feet behind the soldier. He shoved his sword into the man's back and turned to face the next two. The Saint charged to the right, blocking an attack from another enemy soldier, then spun and sliced his opponent in the side, shoving the opponent away with his shoulder. As he spun again, he dropped to one knee, raising his sword and slicing the second soldier in his leg. Knocked off balance, the soldier immediately fell to one knee as The Saint rose to both feet and brought his sword down upon the man's neck, decapitating him.

The Saint readied himself for another attack only to discover all of his enemies fleeing . . . except one. This soldier towered above The Saint. His impenetrable armor showed no weaknesses. He drew a sword that was double the length of The Saint's own weapon, and appeared to weigh more than The Saint could lift. The Saint immediately knew he was no match for this soldier.

"Do you really think you can defeat me?" the soldier taunted.

"The Keeper of The Great City has given me the power to defeat you," replied The Saint with his sword raised. The enemy charged without hesitation, striking with a mighty force that dropped The Saint to the ground. Looming over the fallen Saint, he brought his sword down. The Saint rolled just as the sword came down, the blade burying itself deep in the soft earth rather than the intended target of his head.

"Look at you. You are a weakling! Your sin has made you weak," mocked the enemy soldier.

"I have been forgiven," The Saint replied as he rose to his feet. The enemy soldier yanked his sword from the ground.

"Look at what you have done. Do you really think after all the evil sins you have done you can be useful?" He charged with a deadly swing. The Saint blocked the attack with his own sword and again fell to the ground. "You aren't good enough to be useful," the soldier continued to mock as his sword came down for a final blow. The Saint again successfully blocked the attack and the enemy soldier instantly swung another blow, knocking The Saint's sword out of his hands. The sword flew through the air and stuck into the base of a tree. An evil smirk spread over the soldier's face as he prepared to plunge his sword into The Saint's neck.

"Saint." Someone whispered.

He looked in the direction of the whispered voice. A ghostly figure, who he immediately recognized as the one who had given him shelter the night before, formed right in front of The Saint's sword. The man yanked the sword from the tree, tossed it into The Saint's hand and vanished.

The Saint realized that he couldn't defeat this enemy on his own, but with the help of The Keeper of The Great City, he could do all things. At this realization, his breastplate began to gleam so brightly that everything around him was illuminated. The enemy soldier let out a panicked shout as the blinding light filled his eyes. The Saint swung his sword around and struck the soldier in the back of the leg. The soldier let out another scream as he fell backward. The Saint jumped to his feet.

"I am worthless, but The Keeper has made me worthwhile." The enemy soldier swung a wild swing, and The Saint parried. "I am not holy, but The Keeper has already made me righteous." The soldier swung another wild attack, which The Saint again blocked. "I cannot defeat you, but the Keeper has made me able." With those words, The Saint plunged his sword through the enemy's thick armor, right into his chest.

While retrieving his sword from the dead soldier's body, he heard a noise behind him and spun, ready for another exhausting battle. To his surprise, all of the townspeople stood a few feet off murmuring to one another. The noise quickly grew into loud cheering. He waited for them to quiet.

"The Keeper of The Great City has set you free. You are no longer under the law of the king of this land," he reported as he turned to leave the town.

A young boy about the age of nine ran up to The Saint and pulled on his hand. "I want to be like you! I want to help people and save them from the Evil King," he said. The Saint knelt to face the boy.

"If you are truly serious about serving The Keeper of The Great City as I do, then as soon as we are finished talking, run down that narrow path." The Saint pointed to the path he had come to the village by. The boy's eyes followed The Saint's finger to the dark and foreboding path, his eyes widening as he peered into the dark forest. He stared several long moments into the depths of the forest. Recognizing the fear in the boy's eyes, The Saint gently rested his hands on the boy's trembling shoulders in reassurance. The boy looked back at The Saint. "If you stay on the path, no harm will come to you. The Keeper of The Great City will keep you safe," The Saint assured him in a gentle, calming voice. "Keep going straight until you reach the city I came from. Don't look back, don't stop, and don't leave the path. Now, go." The Saint said, rose to his feet and left the city. The boy turned, looked uncertainly at his parents, then raced down the little path The Saint had directed.

The Saint had traveled the rest of the day peacefully. The path grew more lush and thicker with every step until it was as if The Saint was walking in a verdant tunnel. The night air smelled fresh and cool. The overhanging tree branches blocked out most of the moonlight, making it difficult to see the path. He heard a rustle behind him and spun, withdrawing his sword from its sheath. The little moonlight that seeped through the trees seemed to gather on the blade of his sword and reflect onto the path, illuminating just enough for him to make out the way in the dense brush. Seeing no threat, he continued his journey down the narrow path using his sword's reflection for light. Again, there was a noise, and he froze. Slowly, he turned, scanning the brush around him with his sword. After deciding there was no apparent danger, he apprehensively took a few more steps. Again he heard movement; this time, it seemed to be above him. Something lashed out at him, and he ducked. As quickly as the creature had appeared, it was gone.

The Saint held himself ready for another attack with senses alert and sword raised. The creature struck again, this time at The Saint's feet. He tumbled to the ground, and his sword fell to the side of the path. This time, the attacker did not retreat back into the forest, but taunted him from just a few feet away. The Saint sat frozen as he glimpsed his attacker in the scant moonlight. Terror filled his heart as he looked upon this gigantic serpent. The sight of its leathery skin, the glowing, fiery-red eyes, and deadly teeth pierced into the depth of his soul. The serpent, sensing the fear of his prey, slithered closer until it and The Saint were nose to nose. Horrified, The Saint peered into his tormentor's eyes, eyes that reflected his worn, terror-stricken face. Still paralyzed, The Saint barely noticed the snake coil its giant, leathery body around him. He could think of nothing else but the ferociousness of this massive serpent. The

Saint struggled to breathe and felt the crushing pain of the coiled creature as it began squeezing the life out of him.

The Saint remembered something The City Keeper had told him during his training: "Fear is not of me." The Saint immediately felt a calm begin to overpower his fear. "When you cannot fight, remember my word!" The Saint felt a warm sensation emanating from his belt, then smelled the unmistakable stench of burning flesh. The snake let out a terrible hiss and released The Saint from its grip. The Saint dropped to the forest floor. His belt was glowing a deep red and searing hot, yet astonishingly, it did not affect him at all. He crawled for his sword, reaching it just as the snake angrily reared its head back for an attack. The Saint instinctively rolled onto his back and swung his sword as the serpent struck at him. The sword slashed the serpent's mouth, showering them both with blood. As the serpent leaped for The Saint again, the sword seemed to come alive, deflecting the serpent's attack with a gashing blow to the eyes. The Saint jumped to his feet as the injured serpent recovered. Following the lead of his sword, The Saint spun around, bringing his sword down with a severing blow to the snake's tail. The snake hissed in pain and retaliated in a fit of rage. The Saint planted his feet as his sword rose. The serpent lunged forward, mouth gaping. The sword swung down on its foe's mouth with such power that it forced The Saint into a full spin and sliced open the serpent along its side, then plunged into its belly. The serpent lay dying as The Saint ripped the sword from the creature's stomach. The Saint sheathed his sword with a long exhale of relief.

When The Saint stepped out from the dark forest, he gasped. It was as though he had stepped into a dream world. Beautiful green hills stretched as far as the eye could see. The bright shining moon reflected off crystal lakes and rivers scattered throughout the countryside, amid clusters of lush green trees. Wild beasts roamed freely, and his feet sunk deep into green grass carpeting the ground. In the distance he could see several villages.

The Saint stood a few moments taking in the scenery before he headed toward the closest village. Along the way, he took advantage of the various fruit growing on the trees as he gazed at the night sky in wonderment. As he grew closer to the village, he noticed activity in the courtyard and the faint sound of joyous music. Upon reaching the village, an elderly gentleman stepped out from the side.

"Can I help you, friend?" he asked.

"I am a journeyman and have been traveling a while. I could use a soft bed to sleep in for the night," The Saint replied.

"Where is your journey to?"

"I will know it when I see it."

"Well, journeyman, we are a peaceful city here. You are welcome if you leave your weapons at the door. You will not need them in this place."

"I am grateful." The gatekeeper opened the door and The Saint relinquished his sword and shield.

"Make yourself at home. Help yourself to the food and drink."

"Thanks."

The Saint scanned the area. At the far end of the courtyard stood a buffet table laden with delicious food. A few yards away was a stage on which a band played wind instruments, while in front of the stage the townspeople danced. Spread sporadically throughout the remainder of the courtyard, he saw huddles of people, some talking, others eating, and still others playing all sorts of games.

The Saint made his way to the buffet table and began piling the meat on his plate, then moved on to the vegetables, followed by the desserts, and grabbed a tall cup of water from one of the drink basins. The Saint found an open seat and blessed the meal. As he sat and ate, he simply observed the people as they sang and danced.

"What's your name?" asked a man with a salt-and-pepper beard. The man stretched his hand out, and The Saint shook it as he replied, "Saint."

"Interesting name. I'm Galamiel, the town governor. The older gentleman you met at the gate is Taliel. I hear you are a traveler. See any interesting sights?"

"More than I cared to see."

Galamiel took in The Saint's haggard appearance and battle-worn clothes, grimacing in sympathy.

"Well I just came over to tell you that you're welcome to stay here as long as you want. I have a bed ready for you in my home. Just find me when you're finished." With a friendly pat on his shoulder, Galamiel left.

The next morning, The Saint awoke to the ruckus of children playing. He lay in bed listening to his peaceful and joyous surroundings. An awkward silence descended on the happy village, and The Saint peered out of the window to see what had disturbed the peace. The townspeople had gathered in the courtyard, and The Saint quickly made his way outside to see an older man slowly make his way through the crowd. As he neared the town entrance, the gatekeeper opened the gate and several of the townspeople surrounded the man, and one by one kissed his cheek and squeezed him in their arms. The gatekeeper took the man by the shoulder and lead him out of the town. The Saint called one of the young boys over.

"What's going on?" he whispered.

"We're sending him off to meet the dragon," the boy replied.

"The dragon? For what?"

"So the dragon will have mercy on our town for the next year."

"Why is the gatekeeper going with him?"

"It will be his turn next year. He is to make sure that they get to the dragon's lair."

Horrified, The Saint stood.

"They can't do this!" he said.

"If they don't, then the dragon will kill us all, every village," the boy replied. The Saint peered deep into the eyes of the boy, searching his soul for the horror he himself felt at the situation. He only found acceptance and apathy! Disgust filled his heart as he stared into the innocent little boy's eyes, revealing an empty soul. His face distorted in anger, and he headed for his armor.

The Saint found his armor by the gate and quickly strapped it on as the townspeople scattered, returning to their daily business. The Saint rushed through the gate and scanned the horizon for the two men. What he saw amazed him. The hills were filled with men and women, from every town who had been sent out by their fellow citizens to die. The Saint knew he had to stop this at all costs!

He sprinted in the direction that the townspeople were heading, leaving them far behind. He ran for several hours and the beautiful scenery faded to hard, ugly sulfuric rock.

The Saint finally reached the dragon's lair high in the tallest mountain. He drew his sword and cautiously made his way into the cave. As it grew darker in the cave, his sword grew brighter, filling the darkness with sharp, white light. The cave opened up into a small chamber with several tunnels branching off in all directions. He paused, staring for a moment, unsure which one he should take, then a slight shuffling sound and deep, raspy breathing echoed through the cave.

He had no time to think; The Saint darted into the nearest entrance and covered himself with his shield. The dragon emerged from the tunnel farthest from The Saint and entered into the furthest right, two tunnels over from The Saint's hiding spot. The creature didn't notice the light from The Saint's glowing sword as he passed, and with a sigh of relief, The Saint waited, his palms sweating, for the creature to pass.

He stood a few minutes gathering his courage to face the giant lizard. He had come here for a purpose and that purpose lurked in the tunnels before him. The townspeople depended upon him, whether they knew it or not. With a final prayer for strength and encouragement, The Saint eased out from his hiding hole and followed the dragon through the cave into a large opening.

The Saint jumped out for an attack, his sword raised. His heart raced as he saw the powerful creature's full malevolence and ferocity. Its eyes glowing yellow, the creature snarled and showed its deadly teeth. Smoke billowed out of its nose, and reddish-black scales armored its entire body. It had a tail as large as an oak and legs as thick as a person. Capping its human-sized legs were razor-sharp talons. Its wings spanned its entire body, which The Saint could only guess to be two hundred or so feet.

Seeing its prey, the dragon shot a stream of fire at him. The Saint ducked behind his shield, which quickly heated, burning his arm until he was forced to release his grip. The dragon swung its massive tail, knocking the shield against the wall as The Saint dove over the dragon's tail then rolled to his feet. Realizing his sword would be useless against the giant creature, he flung it to the ground and darted away. The dragon swung its tail around for another attack, and again The Saint dove out of its path. The dragon continued its spin and came abreast with a blaze of fire. The Saint scrambled to his feet and sprinted for a large boulder to shield him from the flames. The Saint could feel the heat at his back as the flames engulfed the rock.

The instant the flames stopped, the dragon slammed its tail into the rock, knocking it into the wall with a loud crash that reverberated off the walls. The tail barely missed The Saint's head as he fell back against the opposite wall. The dragon brought its tail around for another pass as The Saint jumped to his feet and again sprinted wherever his feet wanted to take him. He dropped face first to the ground just as the dragon's tail passed inches above him. Seeing an entrance to another room at his right, he rolled toward it as the dragon shot another stream of flames. The flames barely missed him as he fell down onto a small ledge into the next room, knocking the breath out of him.

The dragon burst through the undersized hole and landed several feet behind him, sending shattered rock flying. The only thing The Saint could think to do was to roll clear of the ensuing landslide, but that placed him directly under the creature's massive belly. The dragon reared up on its hind legs, roaring and smashing its upper body on the cave's ceiling causing several pieces of the ceiling to crumble, then it swung a massive talon at The Saint. The Saint kicked his feet over his head, pushing himself up, and rolled onto his knees as the dragon's massive claws gouged the rock inches from him. The dragon's front leg punched through one of the stone columns supporting the cave. Again, the dragon roared as The Saint hopped to his feet and ran under the dragon as it came down on all four legs with enough force to dislodge more stone from the ceiling. The Saint darted for another stone column as the to enraged dragon swung around, crushing one column with its massive head and smashing its tail through the stone column The Saint was heading for. The Saint dove, barely dodging the dragon's tail.

The rock supporting the columns began to crumble; the cave was collapsing! The Saint jumped to his feet and ran toward the far wall. The dragon thrashed, smashing more rock pillars that supported the cave. The Saint ran up the wall a few steps and jumped with all of his might, dodging a wild swing from the dragon's tail. The dragon roared as it swiveled its neck back and forth, flames blazing.

The Saint noticed another small exit hole and sprinted for it with the wild dragon's fire lapping at his heels. He ducked behind another stone column, narrowly avoiding the deadly flames. The Saint sprinted a few more feet and dove through the small opening as the dragon sped after him. The dragon tried to punch through the small hole, only to make it halfway through. Its arms and legs were trapped, and its midsection caught beneath the jagged rocks that had tumbled down. The dragon frantically struggled to squeeze through, violently swinging its head from side to side.

The Saint searched the cavern for an entrance into the room where he had left his sword and shield. Finally, he found a connecting tunnel that led him back into the room, and he snatched up the items. He slid into the connecting chamber in which the hind end of the struggling dragon lay trapped, and plunged his sword between the dragon's scales.

The dragon roared in pain, angrily smashing into the wall beside The Saint. Yanking his sword out, The Saint dove to the ground and scrambled to avoid being crushed between the dragon's side and the cavern wall. The wall cracked, loosening its grip on the dragon. The dragon, sensing freedom, maneuvered backward, demolishing another stone pillar, then another as it twisted to face The Saint. The cave continued to crumble in on itself as the dragon fiercely smacked its tail into the walls as it charged at The Saint.

The Saint raced for the small exit as he dodged the crumbling stones from the ceiling above as the dragon charged after him, ignoring the rocks pummeling it as the ceiling gave way. The exit to the chamber began to collapse as The Saint dove through it, the dragon right behind him. The ceiling collapsed with a terrible crack of splintering rock on top of the dragon's head. The Saint stood and shoved his sword through the eye of the dragon, piercing its brain, verifying that it was indeed dead. The Saint stared at the massive head for a few moments, grateful that the he had been given the tools to defeat this mighty creature. He turned and left the cave's entrance as the first of the townspeople reached it.

"Go home," he said. "The dragon is dead."

"That's impossible!" said an elderly man who rested against his companion's arm.

"See for yourself," replied The Saint as he turned to climb over the rocky terrain of what was left of the cave's entrance to the mountain top.

When he reached the summit, The Saint was amazed. He knew he had finally reached his destination, for on the other side of the mountain was The Great City.

The Great City was immense and its beauty incomparable. A perfect square spanned an area of twenty-four thousand square miles. The outer wall alone was two hundred feet high and the same thickness. On each wall were three giant pearls that appeared to be the city gates, twelve perfect pearls in all, gleaming in the light. The wall looked as if it were carved out of pure jasper: a smooth glassy surface that glistened a dark forest green studded with precious stones of emerald, topaz, sapphire, amethyst, and others he had never before seen. The Saint felt as if he were looking out into a sparkling forest. From each of the twelve gates stretched streets of pure gold. Gold so pure, so refined, that it was clear as glass. The streets all led to the center of the city forming a square that measured exactly forty square miles. At the middle of this square stood a throne from which twelve crystal clear rivers flowed down the center of each golden street. Trees spanned the streets of gold on either side of the river, bearing twelve kinds of fruit, and a light seemed to emanate from the throne, illuminating the entire city as well as the countryside to where The Saint stood.

He stared in amazement as the glory of The Great City reached out and wrapped him in its welcoming presence, and he knew he was finally home.

TRIN

Lord Trin sat upon his white horse behind the lines of his army on the rise of a large hill with the sun setting at his back, silhouetting his frame. His pure white robes flapped in the wind and cast a long, magnificent shadow across the whole of the valley before him.

The day's battle was nearing its end. The enemy forces were withdrawing, and Lord Trin's own men were shouting in victory at yet another day's battle won. Lord Trin gazed at the scene below. Few of his men had fallen, as always. Yet the valley below was littered with bodies of the fallen enemy like a vast expanse of dead fish afloat on the ocean's surface.

He felt no honor in war and took no pleasure in the deaths of his enemies, but had no choice but to defend his borders. He had given much of his kingdom to this enemy before the war began, back when they chose to leave his rule, back when they were subverted by their own evil desires to follow a rule of anarchy and villainy. Lord Trin had never forced any of his subjects to follow his decrees and was not about to start then. He permitted them unobstructed passage to the edge of his kingdom, and allowed them a permanent dwelling. They soon grew dissatisfied with their own borders, however, and formed a great army and began the war. Lord Trin refused to give any more ground to the dark rebels.

The enemy army massively outnumbered his own men a thousand to one. However, he had never doubted his people's resolve and willingness to fight for their kingdom. His soldiers' armor was superior in every way, and his commander unchallenged in his skills. The enemy army was no match for his, yet they persisted and refused to accept defeat despite the knowledge that it was futile. He could have the enemy wiped out in a day, but refused.

The war was for any who would defect and return to his kingdom and just rule.

Commander Trin pulled his mount up beside Lord Trin. Seated upon their white mounts, the two looked identical, save for Commander Trin who grew no facial hair and that which lay on his head was black as a raven's feathers. He wore no battle armor, only purple robes of royalty, signifying his rank as prince. Lord Trin ignored his son as he pulled up beside him, keeping his attention on the battle scene below, his countenance sorrowful.

"Father, the army awaits your word," Commander Trin stated quietly. Lord Trin nodded and mournfully guided his horse toward his waiting subjects with Commander Trin trailing behind. They pulled their mounts up next to a lone armored warrior who faced the army. Identical to those he commanded, the weapons master wore brightly shining silver armor from head to toe with one addition to his body shield, breastplate, and full face shield; a single cross in gold signified his rank, for no other soldier's armor contained such decoration.

The soldiers fell silent upon Lord Trin and Prince Trin's arrival, awaiting the king's address, which always followed a battle.

"You have fought well today!" Lord Trin began, his voice miraculously carrying over the wind through the entire army, who could all hear Lord Trin with perfect clarity. "Your valor and bravery will be remembered, and you will be blessed in the kingdom after! Stay the course, fight faithfully, and you shall continue to reap the benefits in the kingdom that lies before you. It is difficult, I know, but I promise a great many rewards for you in the kingdom after!

"We have lost some comrades today, nobody feels this sorrow deeper than I, but rejoice in the knowledge that they now reap their rewards with me. Their joy has been made complete! Tonight, we shall remember our beloved departed and rejoice in their splendor, and when you yourselves finally reach that great kingdom in the hereafter, you will find us waiting!" With that, Lord Trin raised his sword high.

"To the fallen!"

A massive roar echoed throughout the sea of bright, metallic armor as all cheered for their fallen comrades. The king sheathed his sword in its scabbard and nodded to his son; the two trotted off into the encampment.

The weapons master waited until Lord Trin and his Commander, Prince Trin had vanished over the hilltop before dismissing the soldiers. In unison the army dropped their shields and unstrapped their breast armor, setting it gently on their shields. Next the rest of their equipment was laid neatly on their shields, each in perfect unison and then they stood, awaiting final dismissal.

The weapons master waved his hand across the formation and the armor vanished at the soldiers' feet. The formation, now dismissed, began breaking up and soon the field stood empty as they made their way to the encampment.

The next morning, Trin arrived on the front defensive lines of the battleground early as a blurry apparition. Lord Trin, Prince Trin, and the weapons master appeared as one, yet individually at the same time. Lord Trin's form appeared in the center of their ethereal formation with both the weapons master and Prince Trin's bodies seemingly to phase in and out as they walked with both appearing in one instant before or behind Lord Trin as the other appeared opposite, then switching positions, and then back again with each passing step.

He called his two best captains to him, Gabriel and Michael, who fell in step behind their Lord. Gabriel and Michael were both young in appearance with pure blond hair, Gabriel's long and Michael's a clean, short cut. Both had bright blue eyes, and though they were battle-hardened, they had soft, fair skin. The three made their way to a large tent in the center of the camp, and Trin led them to a table inside. His ghostly form split into three: the weapons master to his left, and Prince Trin to Lord Trin's right. The trio stood at the edge of the centered table facing their captains. Having witnessed it many times, Gabriel and Michael paid no attention to the sudden division of Trin. Lord Trin then began to tell his two commanders of their plan. The two stood speechless as they listened.

"My Lord," Gabriel replied, "forgive my forwardness, but what you are proposing is madness!"

Lord Trin locked gazes with his commander.

"I am not asking your opinion nor your permission, Gabriel. We will do this, and you will help," Lord Trin chastised.

Gabriel immediately bowed his head slightly.

"Forgive me, my Lord," he replied, knowing he had overstepped his bounds in challenging the wisdom of his Lord.

"Is there any other way, my Lord?" Michael asked.

"I have searched my heart and we have agreed there is no other way," replied Lord Trin.

"And if they discover you?" Michael asked.

"That is inevitable," Prince Trin replied. "However, we have decided it must be done so that one day this war will finally end."

"We will begin preparations immediately, my Lords," Gabriel replied.

Two hours later, Michael led a massive strike to the enemy's furthest and weakest flank in an attempt to distract the enemy army as Gabriel led Prince Trin in a wide arc around the battle grounds, keeping to the ditches and lower portions of the hills. Finally, they passed outside the military district and into the housing section of the city where they neared the enemy's encampment. No sentries or protective walls guarded the borders which were marked by shelters of various shapes and sizes with small breaks in the outer wall.

As they peered into the enemy city through the large gaps in the wall, they could see that many of the outer dwellings were occupied. Children played in the yards, women hung linen or gardened while men kept their fields and farmed their small crops.

Prince Trin and Gabriel slowly crawled their way around the unprotected borders, searching for a good point to infiltrate the enemy city. Soon Prince Trin halted Gabriel, motioning to a young woman who stood hanging her linen.

"She is the one," Prince Trin whispered as he rose.

"My Lord," Gabriel said as he clasped Lord Trin's wrist. "Let me go to her first. Let me ensure your safety." After a moment of consideration, Prince Trin nodded. Gabriel immediately stood tall and slowly walked to the woman, his arms outstretched in a peaceful manner as he passed between the wall sections.

The woman startled a moment as Gabriel neared, then she visibly relaxed as he assured her he meant no harm. Prince Trin watched from afar as the two spoke a moment, until Gabriel returned.

"Farewell, my Lord. Her name is Mary. She is true, and you shall be well cared for by her," he said somberly.

Prince Trin nodded, clasping Gabriel on the wrist and wishing him a farewell as he turned to leave. Gabriel stood, following Prince Trin with his eyes until he disappeared into the woman's home.

Mary and Prince Trin sat in front of her small stone fireplace the rest of the day getting to know each other, talking about nothing at all to very important matters from the day's weather, family and friends, to the future, the city and its inhabitants, and even the meaning of life and the kingdom after. Mary offered him her guest room for as long as he needed it and prepared the beddings for him. He informed her that he needed to speak with others and begin his work, and that they would discuss his plans in the morning. She agreed and the two turned in for the night.

The next morning, Prince Trin woke early and prepared a quick meal. Mary awoke soon after, and the two spent a few minutes eating breakfast and discussing Prince Trin's plans for coming to the city—for any who would choose to follow him. After discussing Prince Trin's plans for the night, Mary ventured through the residences of the city, inviting several of her friends to her house for the midday meal. Due to the short notice, few came.

With Prince Trin's help, Mary prepared the appropriate places for the three guests who promised to come. Soon a young couple, newly married, arrived, followed by a man in his mid-thirties. Mary greeted her friends introducing them to Prince Trin as the simple meal of lamb stew was served.

As the meal concluded, Prince Trin laid his napkin on his plate and stood. He told them that he had come from the great city and that he had come to bring peace to those who would have it and comfort to any who would follow him. He explained that he had come on behalf of the great king beyond to invite their people back into his kingdom. He told them that all he asked was that they profess the great king as Lord and follow His way of life. He informed them that much would be required of those who should choose the way of the great king and that it wouldn't always be easy, but the king would give them the ability to fulfill what is asked of them. He reported that some would be required to give much and others little; of some He would require even their lives. He explained, finally, that all who chose to follow him and the King's ways would never be alone, that Lord Trin will always be with them, and that they would be granted a place with the great king in His Kingdom After.

After a few moments of contemplation, the three each stood proclaiming the great king and accepting whatever fate He would give them. Pleased, Prince Trin began to give a general plan for the next few weeks. The four new citizens of the Great Kingdom brought their own contributions in formulating further plans and strategies for the next few weeks.

Prince Trin and his four followers began covertly spreading news of his arrival. At first, only to their closest friends whom they believed would join their cause. Soon after, many of their friends had converted; they grew slightly bolder, inviting acquaintances and even a few co-workers. Though many did not choose to follow

Prince Trin, there was little concern that they would inform the city guard. Few liked the city guard, and the risk of capture or discovery was minimal to begin with. However, with the growing numbers following Prince Trin, the danger increased and the followers had to begin meeting secretly.

It was during the first of these secret meetings that Prince Trin picked a dozen men to teach his ways on a more intimate level. These twelve would shadow him, learning not only by his teachings but also from his actions and presence. They would become his elite group of followers who would be entrusted with every aspect of his life. He chose these men not by their stature in society, but by the willingness of their hearts. Jonathan, Luke, Markus, Matthew, Lukas, Mark, Joseph, John, Peter, Jude, Philip, and Nathan.

Trin often took these twelve aside after his normal teaching, expounding on his lessons of the day. He gave them additional insights as to why he told the stories he did and explained his actions. He answered their questions more thoroughly than the others and gave them meaningful explanations as to what his stories meant. They became his best friends, rarely separating from the group as a whole and learning much about each other in the process of their tutorship with Prince Trin.

After several weeks of secret meetings, Prince Trin had informed his twelve followers that he intended to begin proclaiming publicly all that he had been teaching to them privately. He chose a small hill along the well-trodden path that led to the city market. Prince Trin's twelve disciples fanned out among the crowd as he began to speak, keeping their eyes and ears open for any sign of the city guard. The crowd quickly grew from his few dozen supporters to a few hundred listeners. He spoke for several hours before the growing crowd caught the attention of the city guard.

The twelve immediately converged on Prince Trin imploring him to flee for fear that the city guard would arrest him for rallying a mob or disturbing the peace. The city leaders disapproved of public gatherings, making examples of perceived rabble-rousers as often as they could.

The city guard reached the small hill on which Prince Trin and his disciples stood only to find it abandoned and its occupants blended into the crowd. The commanding soldier ordered the mob below to disperse at once or they would be detained. The soldier explained that this gathering had not been sanctioned by the proper authorities. The group immediately began to disperse and the soldiers went about their business as Prince Trin met with his disciples privately, discussing a great many things.

Several weeks had passed, and Prince Trin's followers had grown tremendously. He had begun meeting outside the safety of the city walls, among the outskirts of the enemy's land where they kept the outcast, diseased, and poverty-stricken citizens. Few visited these groups for fear of contamination or a simple misconception that they were better than the outcasts, but Prince Trin had no such complex or worries. He knew who he was, and who he came for—*any* who would choose him.

As he had taught this to his followers, many had deserted him not willing to pay the price of their pride. Still others gladly gave over to Prince Trin's philosophy and began venturing out into the outcasts in greater numbers as the days passed by.

Few city guards patrolled outside the city; none enjoyed the outskirts. But several of the city guard had begun to show genuine interest in Prince Trin's teachings and had even approached him in secret.

It was no secret now who Prince Trin was and what he taught, though none, save the few who understood, knew that he was one with the Great King. His disciples, however, still did not grasp fully the meaning of this revelation. Prince Trin now had one of the most recognizable faces in the city. He could no longer hide from those who had voiced publicly their disapproval of his teachings, insisting to the public that he was a criminal and not this righteous man he claimed to be. In truth, they could find nothing solid to convict him with so they had begun plotting ways in which they could capture him. It was not against the law to convene in public, though certain regulations had to be met in advance to meet within the city limits. Now that Prince Trin had begun his meetings outside the city, there could legally be no way to stop him unless he said or did something against the law, a line he was always careful never to cross.

Prince Trin had finished his daily ritual of teaching to the masses and returned into the city and began teaching on a small scale in his followers' houses, as he did often after his public meetings. He always enjoyed this as it was a way for him to teach on a deeper and more personal level. On this particular occasion, Prince Trin had ventured into the home of a new convert and had settled himself into a corner where two dozen followers had joined, sitting on the floor around him. The disciples were scattered among his followers.

Jude and Marcus both stood near the front window listening to Prince Trin's teachings when Marcus accidentally knocked over a clay vase that had been sitting on the windowsill; it shattered with a loud smash and disturbed Prince Trin's teaching. Marcus apologized, explaining that the windowsill was empty when they arrived.

It was then that several of the followers noticed soldiers marching toward the house. Immediately, the congregation began to scatter. Prince Trin and his disciples vanished out the back door as the women raced into the kitchen and the men jumped into the open chairs.

The door burst open and the soldiers barged in, demanding that the criminal Trin be handed over. The gathering insisted that they were merely celebrating the birth of a child, and they had the proper papers. The soldiers searched the house, found no signs of Prince Trin, and left without a word.

Upon leaving the gathering, Prince Trin led his twelve friends deep into the wilderness outside the city walls. At first no one said a word, their nerves rocked by thoughts of their possible fate should they have gotten caught. After a long while and many minutes of walking in utter silence, they began discussing the afternoon's excitement and how that it must not have been mere chance that Marcus had knocked over the vase, which he still insisted he hadn't seen there, upon entering.

They began teasing him unmercifully about the situation, all in good fun, until Prince Trin finally stopped among a grouping of rocks in a small clearing.

They started a fire, as it had begun to grow dark, and Prince Trin finished his teachings to them in great detail. The twelve listened intently on the subjects, especially given the day's circumstances, of provision, trust, love, and sacrifice. Ending with a lesson on sacrifice, Prince Trin announced that he would remain under the stars for the night and that they could all stay or return to the city as they chose. They chose to stay.

The next day was like any other. Prince Trin spoke publicly outside the city to the masses that came to hear his teachings. Most had not devoted their lives fully to him; they still held back things in their hearts, though they had begun to follow his ways. It seemed every day more and more would follow him; even if they were still holding things back in their hearts, they were choosing him, and it pleased Prince Trin.

Prince Trin had great pride, however, in those few who requested to meet with him personally. Even still there were few among those who devoted themselves fully to Him, as he wished all of them would, like his twelve disciples, his closest friends. After his lessons outside the city, Prince Trin again returned to the city and agreed to meet at the house of a young follower who had been showing great interest in his teachings the past few weeks. Prince Trin chose to meet, this time, in the man's backyard which was surrounded by a hedge of vines that concealed them without trapping them. The party of three dozen enjoyed the early evening air as Prince Trin proclaimed his truths to them.

During the middle of Prince Trin's teaching, Jude rushed into the house as he began a coughing fit, not wanting to disturb Prince Trin's lessons. It was growing late, and the first of many stars had begun to shine in the night sky. Prince Trin had just finished the last of his subjects and began saying his good-byes. He was leaving when a loud commotion erupted all around them. Jude burst through the entrance to the house informing the group of several soldiers nearing. Prince

Trin immediately spun as a dozen guards emerged from behind the hedges, surrounding them.

The crowd gathered close together as Prince Trin quietly and casually slipped through a small opening in the hedge where several pots had been placed; his disciples followed. Jude, the last of them to escape as the soldiers' attention were on the large group they had surrounded, accidentally knocked over one of the pots, causing it to crash to the ground with a loud bang. A single soldier noticed yet ignored the fleeing men, turning his attention back to the crowd with a smirk, knowing that his master was indeed safe.

Prince Trin's disciples felt their hearts leap out of their chests when they heard the loud crash as the clumsy Jude knocked the pottery over. Prince Trin ignored the happenstance completely as calm as ever and continued down the street. The twelve reached the safety of Mary's house and immediately began scolding Jude for his clumsiness. Prince Trin, however, reprimanded them and turned their attention to planning the next day's events. Shortly after, they all turned in for the night.

The next morning, Prince Trin woke his twelve friends and set out for the city gates for his daily ritual of teaching. Prince Trin stood on the same small hill until the early afternoon. His disciples mingled with the people. On the outskirts of the crowd several guards patrolled, keeping a keen eye on the growing crowd. A few had merged into the center, truly interested, while most kept close to the outer edges.

Prince Trin stayed all day this time, teaching in the outskirts of the city. The city guard began preparations for closing the city gate as the masses began to migrate into the city. Prince Trin had gathered all his disciples, but Jude who seemed to be nowhere at all. Shortly, Jude revealed himself near a small group where he was talking to several soldiers pointing this way and that, then toward them. The guards nodded and left him be. Jude quickly made his way toward Prince Trin and the other eleven, revealing that the guards have been given orders to apprehend Prince Trin due to testimony that he had broken the law. The Disciples murmured amongst themselves in anger and confusion.

Prince Trin, as was discussed the night before, did not meet with any small groups as he normally did, but led his twelve friends deep into the wilderness to the clearing he had taken them to the other night. Prince Trin fellowshipped with them, then as the others slept, he journeyed deeper into the wilderness to be alone and prepare himself for his upcoming trials.

Late into the night, Jude quietly crept out of the camp and disappeared into the trees. A short time later, the eleven disciples were suddenly awakened as a dozen armed soldiers appeared and dragged them to their feet. The soldiers questioned them, reporting that the gate guards had witnessed a suspicious group, a member of which matched Prince Trin's description, sneak off into the wilderness. After much interrogation, the soldiers finally left them alone as they had no hard evidence that the men were of any threat, and it broke no law to sleep in the wilderness. They let the disciples off with a warning not to be seen with Prince Trin or they would be tried with him. With that, the soldiers left, the band went back to sleep, and Prince Trin appeared upon daybreak to wake them.

Upon hearing the account of the night's activity, he told them he would return to the city. He led the eleven back to the city where they were greeted by a dozen soldiers at the gate. He looked at his eleven friends and told them to stay. He walked to the front gate and stood before the captain of the guard.

To the disciples' astonishment, Jude appeared from behind the crowd of soldiers. They could barely make out the words but knew enough to understand Jude had given testimony of a crime Prince Trin hadn't committed. The soldiers led Prince Trin into the city as Jude glanced back at the eleven who stood together in the distance then he entered the city, his head low and his heart troubled, never to be seen again by anyone.

Three days had passed and Prince Trin's followers had forsaken him. Those who had come to listen to Prince Trin on the hill outside the city simply returned to their business as if he had never been. Those who had often sat with him in their homes quickly forgot his teachings, returning to their old ways of life, and his closest friends, forever changed as they would be, returned to their empty lives going about their now empty days sullenly.

On the evening of the third day, a commotion broke out in the housing district of the city as a man strolled down the street with a woman by the name of Mary. He looked familiar, yet none could place where they had known him from, yet as they saw the familiar man, they felt an unexplainable need to follow. He was on his way to meet some old friends, and invite them for one last walk before he left. A crowd had gathered behind him as those who had seen him began to follow.

The man reached the first of his destinations, the house of one of his closest friends. He knocked on the door and turned to leave without waiting for an answer. When Nathan came to the door, known to all as one of the twelve, he saw the familiar man and rushed up beside him, again with that unexplainable need to follow him. The familiar man greeted him and continued to the houses where Peter, John, Philip, and Joseph lived. He then led his five friends and Mary into the business section of the city where he found the remaining six disciples. Soon, the eleven and Mary, along with a massive following behind, marched outside the city where the eleven had finally recognized the familiar man as Prince Trin!

They surrounded him with hugs and kisses, requesting in excitement that he tell them how he had escaped. Finally, Prince Trin explained that he had not escaped but had faced the full punishment for his "crime" as he had intended before he ever came into their land. He told them that he was going back home, and soon they would all be able to come, but first they had to carry on his teachings to the rest of the city dwellers. He told them that it would be difficult, yet more fulfilling than anything they could imagine. He explained that any who chose to devote themselves completely to him would require much dedication, even their lives if necessary. He assured them that he would always be with them in their hearts and that he looked forward to their next meeting. With that, he reentered the city, crossing through the city and into the military barracks, then out the front military gate into the night.

Lord Trin and the weapons master stood silhouetted against the rising sun watching in anticipation as Prince Trin finally returned home. They observed him as he journeyed from the enemy camp, across the battlefield, and up the hill on which they stood.

"It is finished," Prince Trin reported. He glanced back and saw the first of his disciples coming home, leading half a dozen behind him. He knew there would be converts returning home for all time, until they decided to end the war once and for all—but that was another matter. For now, the war would continue though it has already been won, and more would return home. Prince Trin turned and disappeared behind the hill. The three merging into one ethereal form, their work done!

OMEGA STATION

Jack Byron and Alyssa Houston stepped through the airlock into the space station Omega and scanned the heavily trafficked plaza. Entrances into small shops and restaurants lined the walls. One such restaurant had a bar window running along its wall with half a dozen stools seemingly there for looks only. In the center of the plaza stood an information booth, while overhead spanned walkways that connected to another floor that housed the main restaurant; it was aesthetically designed as the hub of the station with tables overlooking the lower level. A stairway spiraled up to the center of the food court just above.

"Guys, it's about time you got here!" Jack and Alyssa spun around to see Silas Enders sauntering toward them. "You guys hungry?" he asked after hugging them in turn.

"Seven hours on a third class shuttle, you bet we're hungry," Jack answered. "I hear Courtney's is a good place."

The three entered Courtney's and sat at the bar.

"May I help you?" asked the bartender, a beautiful, black-haired woman.

"Can we get a table for three in the balcony? My friends just arrived. It seems your reputation has preceded you again," Silas answered.

Courtney smiled and waved an available server over. Moments later they were seated at an outside table overlooking the plaza. They took their time over the meal, catching up and reminiscing about their first years in the academy before the conversation turned to current events, the station, and the Hamari.

The Hamari were a group of renegades that had been exiled from their home planet, Hamar, for attempting to overthrow the government nearly a century before. Since that incident, they had been stirring up trouble for the Space Core Alliance. They had grown in numbers over the years. And had become skilled thieves and saboteurs raiding countless Space Core Alliance ships and generally wreaking havoc.

"This station is in the middle of nowhere," Silas said. "The most excitement we ever see is a few minor skirmishes from nearby planets and the occasional unruly drunk. The Hamari have no interest in this station. Why do you think the Space Core Alliance allowed shopkeepers and civilians to come out here? This station is insignificant compared to the new battle station."

"That's what I'm talking about," Jack replied. "That station is less than a day from here at top speed. If someone, like the Hamari, want to take that station, or get the slightest advantage, they might try it from here. Think about it; if someone wanted the station, they could go through the back door: us. Even if we have the most advanced station in the galaxy, we are still vulnerable."

"Look," Silas retorted, "with the battle station such a short distance away no one would dare try to take us. We would have reinforcements before they could even get the ships in position. You forget we have the most advanced defensive equipment. It's impenetrable."

"Yeah, defenses for ship attacks, but what about an attack from within?" Jack countered. "Look at all of the civilians. Do we really want their blood on our hands if something does happen?"

"Jack, all of these people signed the forms stating they know the risks of living on this station." He leaned into the table drawing breath to launch further arguments when Alyssa interrupted.

"I'm sorry to stop the fun, but it's getting late, and I'm going to bed. See you guys tomorrow."

"She's right. I should turn in myself. See you later, Silas." Jack jumped up from the table and jogged to catch up with Alyssa.

"So what do you think about the probability of an attack?" he asked her.

"I think Silas has a point. I don't think, with the station so close that anyone will try to attack us, but the argument you put up raised a very good point. We are the perfect target for an attack from within.

Maybe we have people in our own security that are on the other side, or the bridge officers, or even the shop keepers are spies," she responded jokingly. They both smiled and said their good nights.

Beep! Beep! Beep! Jack's alarm woke him up at five thirty in the morning. Groaning he rolled out of bed and staggered to the shower. Fifteen minutes later, he was wide awake, in his uniform and ready to go. Realizing he had some time to kill before his shift, he decided to see if breakfast was being served. As he suspected, Courtney's was not yet open, but he could smell fresh muffins at a small restaurant a few stores down the plaza and was compelled to check it out. He slid into the first booth, and ordered black coffee, scrambled eggs, and buttered toast.

"Is this seat taken?"

Jack looked up to see a sleepy-eyed Alyssa standing before him. "Eggs and toast with coffee. Is that it?"

"I'm not much of a big breakfast eater. What about you? Eaten yet?"

"Yeah, I had eggs in my quarters. I was just taking a walk around the station, getting to know the layout. I saw you sitting here and thought I'd keep you company."

"Well, thanks."

"No problem." She dropped into the booth across from him and the two chatted for a few minutes while he finished his coffee.

"Isn't it strange that the two of us both got the same assignment?" she asked as they were leaving.

Jack didn't answer but gave a little smile. They turned into the security office, and Jack reached for the daily routine clipboard.

"Let's see where our first stop is today. Inspect cargo bays in levels one through six. Great!"

Silas arrived a few seconds later, and they left to get an early start on their rounds. When they finished, all three of them headed to Courtney's for lunch.

"Check it out," Jack said, nodding in the direction of a young black man who was standing at the restaurant entrance. Silas and Alyssa both followed his nod.

"Is that Gabriel?" Alyssa asked.

"Yeah, I think so. Let's invite him over," Silas suggested as he stood, but Alyssa grabbed his arm.

"Wait a minute. Gabriel bugs me, always talking about God and stuff."

"Oh, come on, Alyssa!" Silas protested. "He has never pressed you with his religious beliefs!"

With that, he pulled away and invited Gabriel to join them. The four chatted for a while, then the three security officers headed back to work for their second assignment of the day.

"Hold on. I left the clipboard in the last cargo bay we checked," Jack said, motioning for them to follow.

They entered the cargo bay, and Jack was almost knocked off his feet by a technician rushing out the door.

"Watch where you're going," Jack ordered, but the man ignored him as he flew by.

"Wonder where he's in such a hurry to get to?" Silas remarked.

Suddenly, all three officers stopped in mid-stride as they noticed a large crate broken open with a clear liquid seeping out of the bottom.

"Get him!" Jack ordered, and Silas and Alyssa immediately raced after the stranger.

Jack radioed for a hazmat crew on his wrist communicator then studied the contents of the crate as he waited for them to arrive. The crate contained Caltarian eggs, an extremely dangerous animal from Caltaria, a very dangerous planet. A vicious animal indeed and used primarily for sport by skilled hunters. The eggs were covered with a clear gelatin. When the hazmat crew arrived, they carefully secured a sample and handed Jack the specimen jar.

In the lab, Jack stood with several of the technicians.

"I've never seen anything like it," said one of the lab officers as he examined the egg and gelatin under a large microscope.

"The gel seems to have fertilized the egg, and the egg itself is growing at an exponential rate. The embryo has definitely been mutated somehow." The lab officer stepped back and erected a force field around the equipment.

"I'll patch this microscope into the computer so we can watch it on the screen. We need to contain the rest of these where they are. Don't let anyone near the cargo bay."

"We have a hazmat team securing the area with several of my personnel guarding the entrance," Jack assured him.

The lab technician nodded and glared intently at the microscope screen trying to make sense of it.

"We've got to figure out what this thing is or is going to be." He turned to Jack. "You said you caught someone fleeing from the scene. I need him."

Jack nodded and called for Silas and Alyssa to bring the detainee to the lab. When they got there, the suspect was squirming wildly. Jack grabbed his face to still him.

"What were you doing in the cargo bay, and what are those eggs?" he asked.

"Nothing," the suspect answered. "I was making sure my cargo had gotten there ok. I saw the eggs, and I took off."

"Liar! What were you doing? We know the eggs have been altered. Why were you sabotaging them? What scam are you trying to pull?"

"We've got it," one of the lab workers reported as the main screen switched to the inside of the egg.

The crook's eyes widened in horror as the screen viewed the creature. Almost instantly, the egg burst open, hurling pieces of the microscope into the surrounding force field.

"Where'd it go?" shouted the lab director anxiously.

All eyes searched inside the force field looking for the tiny creature.

"There!" Jack pointed to a small hole in the floor just under the microscope. "It looks like it cut its way out."

The head lab officer shut the shield off and knelt down by the hole.

"It looks like someone took a can opener to the hatch and forced it open. It must have chewed its way through. There's saliva all around the edges," he reported.

Suddenly, the man's eyes widened as the creature jumped out of the hole onto his face, knocking him back into the wall as the creature ferociously attacked and disappeared into his chest. Blood poured from the dead man's body and onto the floor around him. The three security officers pulled out their guns and trained them on the corpse.

The man in custody took advantage of the confusion and darted away. Jack ignored the fleeing criminal and cautiously inched up to the dead man and pulled the body so that it fell flat. Again the creature had ripped through the vent. Jack spoke into his wrist communicator ordering security to cargo bay 16. Jack turned to Alyssa and Silas.

"Alyssa, you go to the bridge and tell them we've got to evacuate the station immediately. Silas, try to find that creature and kill it before it kills anybody else. Let's all pray that the rest of those eggs haven't hatched yet." Jack finished and was the first one out the door.

Three security officers stood waiting outside cargo bay 16 as Jack reached the hall.

"When I open the door, be ready to fire at anything that moves. And I mean anything." He opened the door and to his relief, none of the eggs had hatched yet. But just as the four lowered their weapons, several eggs burst open with a flurry of motion and the creatures clung to the ceiling. Immediately, the three officers behind Jack began firing at the creatures hanging from the ceiling as he punched the button to close the door.

"Come on!" he ordered and began to sprint down the hall. Again he spoke into his communicator. "Code Red, Code Red, Alpha, Omega, and Beta teams to the armory."

Just as he was speaking, the red emergency lights flickered on and an emergency evacuation alarm sounded.

As Jack and the three officers with him raced through the corridors and through the plaza, all but the three security teams ordered to the armory were desperately trying to keep the evacuees calm as they all headed for the escape pods. Once in the artillery room, Jack briefed the awaiting officers on the situation.

"Keep these creatures away from the civilians until they are all evacuated. Once they're safe, then we can worry about ourselves, understood?"

They all nodded an affirmative.

"Alpha team, you stay on the top level in case any of these creatures get through. Omega, you go through every corridor and make sure everybody is out; if you run into any of those creatures, shoot to kill. Beta team, you're with me."

Jack spun and immediately the security officers all shuffled into their designated groups and set out to accomplish their missions.

Beta team rounded the corner right into an onslaught of the now fully-grown creatures. For the first time, Jack got a good look at the horrific creatures: insect-like, their skeletons were on the outside. A dark gray with talons that looked as if they could rip through a person in a seconds and their triangle shaped head with huge, evil, bug eyes, and an elongated mouth full of razor-sharp teeth loomed above from the imposing height of nearly ten feet. All the officers stared aghast. The creatures spotted them.

"Fall back!" Jack ordered as the creatures charged.

The team immediately withdrew around the corner and down the corridor. Jack stopped at a security panel and punched in the force field code just in time. The creatures slammed into the force field and fell to the floor. Leaning against the wall, Jack let out a sigh of relief.

"That was close," he said as he stared a few moments at the vicious creatures who had regained their feet and were slamming into the force field.

The officers secured the next to last escape pod as the remaining civilians filed into the pod and waited for the last of their comrades to return. Several dozen security personnel stood guard throughout the shopping plaza with Jack, keeping a keen eye out for the creatures. Simultaneously, their security wrist communicators jumped to life: "This is Ensign Rogers to any and all personnel. The creatures are on the move. At least a dozen and we've got civilians coming your way. We need back up here!"

"Location?" Jack requested through his wrist intercom.

"North East Corridor, level one!"

Jack motioned for Alyssa and Silas to follow him and they raced toward the stranded team.

They rounded the corner to find several young children screaming and half a dozen of the creatures slaughtering the security officers.

"Alyssa, get these kids out of here!" Jack ordered as he and Silas opened fire. They killed two of the creatures before they retreated. No matter how fast they ran, the creatures quickly gained on them. They could feel the breath of their pursuers on their necks as they entered the plaza and knew they were dead.

Explosions erupted dangerously close to the two, sending them sprawling to the ground. The smell of charring flesh the horrifying screeches of the aliens filled the air. They quickly rolled to their backs, weapons at the ready only to find the alien creatures engulfed in flames just feet away. Satisfied the alien threat was momentarily neutralized and very much relieved they had survived, they scanned the area for any remaining threats and were amazed to see Courtney, the bartender, standing against the wall holding several glass bottles.

"My own concoction," she said with a sly smile. "Works great."

"You should be in one of the pods. What are you doing?" Silas demanded as he and Jack clambered to their feet without even a hint of gratitude for their rescuer.

"I forgot a few things," she replied flippantly, shrugging her shoulders.

"Like what?" Jack asked.

She held up a data stick.

"That's worth risking your life for?"

"If you've just struck it rich it is. As soon as I get somewhere safe, I'm going to cash it all in."

"Congratulations, but let's try to get somewhere safe first," Silas suggested.

"Well, help me with these bottles then, boys," Courtney ordered.

They each grabbed two bottles and headed for the escape pods.

Alyssa had just finished securing the children in their seats when one little boy started hollering. Alyssa was at his side in an instant

"What's the matter?"

The boy frantically reported that his sister was gone. Darting from the pod, she scanned the area. The boy's sister had somehow made her way up onto the balcony. Alyssa rushed up the spiral stairs and across the walkway. The instant she grabbed the girl, an alien creature leapt from the shadows directly in front of her. Alyssa stumbled and flipped over the rail. She grabbed onto the underside of the walkway, still awkwardly holding onto the little girl while she tried to evade the creature as it leaned over the railing. Suddenly it fell overboard, and she heard a voice.

"Give me the girl."

With relief, Alyssa looked up to see Gabriel's arms outstretched and she gladly handed the little girl to him before pulling herself up.

"What happened?" she asked when she regained her composure.

"Remember me telling you about my archery trophies?"

Alyssa nodded.

"Well, I always knew that stuff would come in handy."

Gabriel pointed to the dying creature, an arrow protruding from its eye.

"Come on, let's get out of here before more of these creatures come."

Alyssa escorted the little girl into the pod and secured her into the seat before launching the pod out into space where it joined the parade of departing civilians. Finally, the security officers started strapping themselves in just before they shut the doors; however, the power flickered and partially returned.

"Looks like they attacked the generator. Let's get out of here," Alyssa said as she pressed a switch. But just as the door began to shut, everything went completely black. A fearful murmuring spread through the cabin.

"Everybody, stay calm!" Jack yelled. "This is just like all those exercises, remember? Get the flashlights from the survival kits under the seat."

Seconds later, the darkness was pierced by several dozen flashlight beams all trained on Jack who brought up a hand to block the blinding light. The lights quickly lowered as the handlers realized they had blinded him.

"Okay. Listen up. We all know that the life support is on a separate system from the regular and the backup systems. Now the aliens couldn't have done this, which means either we still have someone on board sabotaging the station, or more likely, someone downloaded a virus into the station's systems. We have got to reboot the system from the bridge.

"Alpha and Beta, follow Silas and guard the pad. Alyssa, take Gamma and Delta teams. Go to engineering and see if you can find a way to get the life support back on. Omega and Theta teams, we're headed to the bridge. When the power comes back on, everybody makes their way back. Nobody leaves until we're all accounted for, dead or alive, understood?"

The entire force simultaneously responded, "Yes, sir!"

"Let's move."

Immediately, the selected teams divided and left. Jack turned to Courtney and Gabriel.

"You guys wait here, find a weapon in case those things come looking for food."

"Don't worry about us, Jack." Gabriel smiled. "We can take care of ourselves."

"Well, the same old Gabe." Jack patted him on the shoulder and spun around.

Jack and his team, as quickly as caution would allow made their way through the first of the many corridors heading for the bridge. They were a few feet from the corner when a severed head rolled into their path and every officer trained their weapon on it. An alien rounded the corner to fetch the head, but the security officers opened fire before it could rip the flesh from the bone.

When they ceased fire, the horrifying sound of a dozen aliens echoed down the corridor.

"Fall back!"

Jack ordered unnecessarily because before he could even finish the word, the squad had already begun to retreat.

Again, the aliens chased them to the force field; however, before it could be erected, one of the creatures got through. Blood sprayed everywhere as the creature dug its teeth into first one, then another unfortunate officer, while the rest of them unloaded their rounds on it. It was dead within seconds. Blood splattered the walls, ceiling, floor, and was soaked into their uniforms. Jack checked the pulse of the two victims. He shook his head and began doubling back.

"Get their weapons," ordered Rimerez, the captain of Omega team. He ran to catch up with Jack.

"Sir, if the power is out, how did that force field work?"

"The force fields have their own power generators; they are not part of the actual system."

Rimerez nodded and fell back into step behind Jack.

"So . . . you a Christian?" Courtney asked as she and Gabriel sat, awaiting the others' return.

They were propped against her bar. Gabriel had his bow across his lap, while bottles of Courtney's brew sat by her side.

"Yup. I sure am."

"Huh."

"What's wrong? You've got something against believing in God?"

"No. It's just that all the Christians I've known are hypocrites."

"Well, I've always said there are two kinds of Christians: there's the hypocrite and there's the hypocrite." The corner of his mouth quirked up at his own joke.

"What do you mean by that?" Courtney asked, intrigued despite herself. She cocked her head to get a better look at Gabriel.

"The first kind of Christian say they are Christians, and then act just like they did before they were saved. Then there are the Christians who get saved and turn from their past ways: Because of our sinful nature, however, no matter how Christ-like we try to be, we always end up a hypocrite because we sin too."

"Well, given your descriptions I would have to agree," she said with a slight smile.

Gabriel's face grew serious.

"You said you know a lot of Christians, but what do you think about Christ?"

"If you're referring to Jesus and the story of how he died on the cross for our sins, rose again, and that if we just believe in him, confessing our sins, we will be saved. I just don't get it. Why he would die for me? I mean, if you knew some of the things I've done." Her eyes filled with remorseful recollection.

"You know, I used to have the same problem as you," Gabriel admitted. "I used to think God couldn't love me because of the horrible things I'd done. Then someone told me of a man who murdered Christians, and Jesus forgave him. It was the story of Saul of Tarsus, also known as Paul, that reached me."

"Everyone says you are just the nicest guy. What could you possibly have done?" Courtney asked.

Gabriel paused a moment, his eyes peering deep into her own.

"I was a hired killer. If someone paid me enough, I would kill whoever they wanted. They finally caught me, and I was sent to prison where I found Christ."

Courtney's eyes widened in shock.

"Because I'm not proud at all of what I did, I hardly talk about that part of my life. Those people could be in hell because of me."

"I'm sorry. I had no idea."

"That's all right. That's why I told you. I just hope I can change your view on Christianity."

Suddenly the quiet was shattered by loud gunshots.

Alyssa was the first in sick bay. Immediately, she began pumping the manual door lever as her team poured through. She waited as long as she could before closing the door fully, knowing that if she waited until everybody was in there was a good chance some of those creatures would get in as well. There were still two officers trying to get to the door. Alyssa took one last look before closing the doors and saw one of the aliens snatch up the last officer as if the woman weighed nothing. Seconds later, she heard the dying screams of a fellow officer as he slammed against the other side of the door. The room became silent except for the dozen or so creatures clawing at the door.

"How many did we lose?" Alyssa asked.

"Five. Hutch, Sterling, Casio, Bernard, and Larson," reported one of the officers.

Struggling to keep the emotion from her face, Alyssa unlatched the maintenance tube hatch.

"We can get to engineering through here," she said as she crawled in, leading the way. She pushed the horrific screams of the last officer she had sacrificed out of her mind.

Jack led his team through a maze of tubes and straight into an alien nest.

"Holy, Mary, mother of God."

"Sir, what's wrong?" asked Rimerez.

"Our problems just got worse. We just ran into an egg hive."

"Great, it's going to take forever to backtrack."

"No. We have to go through, there's no telling how many of these creatures have already hatched, and we need to get this station on line."

Jack cautiously led his team around the egg sacks and through the tube.

All but the last three officers had made it through the next junction when the egg sacks began bursting open. The first officer hurled himself into the corresponding tube as the last two scrambled for the junction. One officer let out a terrified scream as a dozen newly hatched aliens began to rip the flesh from his body. His mind, twisted with fear and pain, wouldn't allow him to think clearly. He let go of the rails and tumbled down the tube. The second officer was almost at the junction when one of the creatures latched onto his back. Instinctively he reached for the alien as another latched onto his arm. Just as he began to fall a crewmate grabbed his arm and pulled him through the hatch as another dangerously shot the alien from his back as the other leapt from his arm. They quickly closed the hatch behind him as another alien leapt toward them.

Silas dove over the bar window into Courtney's just as the security bars lowered. "Stowker, how many did we lose?" he asked as he rolled to his feet.

"Over half, sir." Silas plopped onto a stool at the front bar.

"Silas, we can't do anything more for them now. It's time for them to answer to their Creator," Gabriel said. "We need to worry about those that are still living. It's not going to be too long before these creatures break through."

Silas jumped back to his feet as one of the aliens slammed into the bars, slightly bending them.

"Holy cow," Stowker said.

Courtney popped up from behind the bar.

"Guys, I think I've found a way out." She showed them a hole in the wall, behind a shelf of wine bottles and pulled several illegal drinks out. "It's where I stash my illegals, I just thought of it, and it might get us somewhere safer."

Silas unstrapped his security belt and rifle and handed them to Gabriel.

"I'll go in and see where it leads. Don't tell anyone about this. I don't want to get their hopes up only to disappoint them."

"Sir? You're not going to take your weapon?" Stowker asked.

"It'll slow me down. I've got to get back before these creatures get in." With that, Silas crawled through the opening and disappeared.

Courtney unshelved a bottle of brandy and poured herself a drink.

"If you guys want some, help yourselves. It's not like there's anything else to do," she said.

"Do you have anything non-alcoholic?" Gabriel asked.

"There are some exotic juices I use to mix drinks next to the brandy."

Gabriel hopped over the counter and poured himself a glass of juice.

"So you never told me whether you believe in Jesus or not," Gabriel said.

"I believe in God, but I'm not so sure about all that Jesus stuff."

"Let me just ask you this question. Let's just say there's two people, one is a Christian, and the other is just a man who believes in God, but never gave his life to Christ. Both these men live their lives and die. If what the Bible says doesn't really matter, then the Christian goes to heaven as well as the other guy. Now, what if the Bible is true? The Christian goes to heaven and the unsaved guy goes to hell and burns forever. Are you willing to take the chance of going to hell?"

Courtney sat in silence for a few seconds.

"If the Bible is true, no."

"Okay. You said you believe in God, right?"

She nodded.

"If there was, and there is, only one way to get to heaven, don't you think God would show us that way?"

"Well . . . sure."

"And wouldn't you think the easiest way to tell you would be to write it down and send a messenger to give the letter to you?"

"I guess."

"So wouldn't it make sense that God would send a messenger, Jesus Christ, to come to earth and show us the way?"

Courtney didn't say a word but seemed to be staring off into space, and Gabriel knew God was working.

"So if the messenger came and delivered the message, don't you think God would have recorded that message in a letter?"

Still no answer. Gabriel took Courtney's hand.

"Courtney, that message is in this book." He pulled a small pocket-sized Bible from his trouser pocket. "And that message contains the only way to heaven. Won't you read the message?"

Again, Courtney nodded a yes, and Gabriel read the scriptures to Courtney, giving her his Bible to follow along in.

"First, Courtney, you must realize and admit that you are a sinner. You see, the Word of God states in Romans 3:23, 'For all have sinned and fall short of the glory of God.' And because of our sin, we cannot be with God. Now, do you admit that you have sinned?"

"Yes."

"Okay. Let's go on. Romans 6:23 says, 'For the wages of sin is death, but the gift of God is eternal life in Christ Jesus our Lord!' Now this is not talking about physical death, but spiritual death. The Bible states that after we die, we will either go to heaven or hell. This verse is speaking of hell, the second death. Thankfully, this verse also states the gift of God is eternal life, which brings us back to Romans 5:8, 'But God demonstrates his own love for us in this: while we were still sinners, Christ died for us!' You see, Courtney, God loved you enough to send his only son so you could be with him in heaven. You said you are familiar with the account of Jesus dying on the cross for our sins, even though he was free from sin himself. When he died he paid the price for our sin. When he rose again, he conquered death. Now, let's turn to Romans 10 verses 9, 10, and 13, 'That if you confess with your mouth, Jesus is Lord, and believe in your heart that God raised him from the dead, you will be saved. For it is with your heart that you believe and are justified, and it is with your mouth that you confess and are saved. For everyone who calls on the name of the Lord will be saved!'

"These scriptures say that if you believe that Christ rose from the dead and confess with your mouth you will be saved. Courtney, you've already admitted you are a sinner. Do you believe that Jesus Christ is Lord and rose from the dead?"

Courtney looked up at Gabriel with tears in her eyes.

"Yes."

"Then I want you to pray this prayer with me: Dear Lord, I know I am a sinner and can't get to heaven on my own. I need you to come into my heart and save my soul that I may live forever with you in heaven. Amen."

Courtney repeated every word after him.

Silas returned from the secret tunnel.

"Okay. Everybody listen up. We've found a way out of the present danger. Follow Officer Winters through the tunnel. Don't rush, stay in single file. Several officers will stay behind to protect you as long possible."

"Creeger, Smith, Jones, Parkinsins, and Summers, you're with me. Oliver, keep that line moving." Silas and the five officers kept alert as the rest of the group crawled through the tunnel.

The creatures seemed to sense that their prey was escaping and began to charge the bars more frantically. The last officer entered the tunnel, and Gabriel hollered to the guarding officers to fall back. They began their retreat as one of the aliens squeezed its way through the broken bars. The alien charged at its closest prey, falling to the floor as the officer fired his weapon, but not before it managed to gash deep cuts into the officer's chest.

Silas rushed to help as another alien squeezed through the bars. With one arm, Silas trained his weapon on the creature and fired his last rounds into it, causing little damage to the alien creature while with his other hand, he helped Officer Jones to his feet. Silas threw his useless gun down and prepared to die, but just before the creature reached him, Gabriel dove over Silas' back onto the alien's neck. The sudden impact knocked the alien off balance and slammed it to the floor. The creature squirmed, trying to fling Gabriel off and get to its feet.

"Get . . . out . . . of . . . here!" he shouted, exasperated as he bounced through the air.

Silas dragged Officer Jones to the tunnel and turned back for one last look as his friend screamed in horrific pain when a second alien teamed with the first and began tearing the flesh from his body and his blood sprayed everywhere, dribbling down the creatures' mouths and puddling at their feet. The aliens finished devouring Gabriel and charged for Silas, but he dove into the tunnel, pulling Officer Jones with him.

The last of Jack's team dove through the cargo bay doors as they closed. "Okay. Here's the plan," Jack said. "We lower the force fields and open the doors to space. We'll blow those suckers out into space."

"What about us? How will we keep from being blown into space? That vacuum is too strong for anyone to hold onto anything," Officer Jennings protested, concerned.

"Look around, there should be safety harnesses near the consoles or walls. Strap into them. If there aren't enough then rip out the wiring to some of the consoles and tie yourselves to something stationary. Let's get moving."

The group secured themselves with harnesses, or with gutting the consoles, securing themselves to anything that wouldn't get blown out into space.

"Remember to let the air out from your lungs. Don't hold your breath or your chest will explode. Get ready . . . 3 . . . 2 . . . 1 . . . depressurizing," Jack said.

At that moment, the officer closest to the corridor door yanked the lever to open the door. It slid open mere inches, and the aliens began tearing and ripping through the doors forcing it even wider. Any fixtures not bolted down blew into the oblivion of space along with all the aliens as the force of the wind ripped the officers away from their positions and blew them toward the black abyss. Their security straps stretched to their limits and they immediately began to feel the effects of the lack of oxygen. Their lips started turning blue and they started to feel tingling then dizziness and a pounding headache. Only a few seconds had passed and the creatures continued to fly past the security team and into space, their appendages flailing. Finally, the last of the aliens were blown out into space. Jack struggled against the force of the wind blowing against him as he reached for the button to re-pressurize the cargo bay. He fought through the dizziness and massive headache, and wrestled with his own inability to focus. His coordination worsened by the second as his mind hungered for oxygen. Finally he clumsily pressed the button to re-pressurize the cargo bay.

Alyssa popped her head out of the maintenance tunnel.

"It's clear. Let's go," she ordered as she crawled out.

She and the first officers out stood lookout as the rest of the team emerged from the tunnel.

"Engineering is three levels down. The quickest, and probably safest, way is through the elevator shaft just around the corner."

Alyssa led the way to the shaft and waited until the last of her team was in before taking up the rear. After a long climb down, the team gathered at the shaft entrance, readying their weapons in case of attack from any of the three conjoining corridors.

"Clark, Williams, Ryder, secure the right corridor. Wilson and Daniels, you're with me. The rest of you, prepare to back us up, and get that door open," Alyssa ordered.

"Ma'am."

"Yes, Cyphers?"

"I just thought I might inform you that we're almost out of ammo."

Alyssa looked at her clip.

"Same here," she replied. "Hurry it up over there."

Silas hopped out of the tunnel into the room with the other officers.

"Make sure no aliens get through that tunnel alive, and get Jones some medical attention."

"Where's Gabriel?" Courtney asked.

"He's dead."

Courtney fell against the wall. Silas rested a hand on her shoulder, sorrow evident in both their eyes as he walked past her and slid open the exit door. An opening just big enough for one person to crawl through was revealed. He cautiously made his way through the opening and emerged behind a false air vent tucked into a corner so that to the normal passerby it seemed as if he had just rounded the corner. He quickly scanned the area as he made his way into the open, motioning to the others to come out. One by one the officers emerged guns held steady.

Jack and his team successfully made it the rest of the way to the bridge.

"Everybody pick a station and inspect it for anything out of the ordinary," he ordered.

The team began searching the consoles inside and out.

"Sir, I found something," Rimerez reported, and Jack strode to his side. "It's just above the cooling system."

Sticking his head in the bowels of the console, he saw a tiny black cylinder.

"Looks like it was fused into the actual circuit board. I've never seen anything like this. It must contain the virus that affected the central computer."

Suddenly, the light burst on so brightly it blinded the officers before flashing off again.

"What did you do?" Rimerez asked.

"I didn't do anything," he replied as he disentangled himself from under the console. "Rimerez, you stay here and work on getting the power back on. Butters, Wallace, and Robins, help him. Anyone with serious wounds, Mr. Jennings will do what he can for you. The rest of you, we're leaving," Jack ordered, dread rising in the pit of his stomach.

He led his team off the bridge and down the corridors until they came upon the last known location of the alien creatures. The security team rounded the corner, expecting a confrontation, only to find the nauseating sight of half-melted and dying aliens on the ground, along with the penetrating smell of searing flesh in the air.

"Disgusting," Officer Wilkins said. "That smell . . . what happened?"

"The lights fried them," Jack explained. "That's why they burst on so brightly."

"Well, that's good, right?" Wilkins asked.

"No. Not at all. There's only one possible explanation. Someone wants this station and will be coming to claim it. We can't let that happen, and there's no telling how long it will be before they board."

Jack turned to three officers. "Get to the armory and prepare everything, right down to the last clips. Now."

"Yes, sir," Wilkins replied as he and Officers Potter and Providence raced to the armory.

The light exploded on, blinding Alyssa and what was left of her team. The aliens screeched ear-bursting screams as their blood began to boil in their veins and flesh melted from their bodies. The lights blackened again, and slowly the security officers regained their vision.

They observed their surroundings in amazement as they saw the remains of the deadly creatures. Alyssa began to help the injured to their feet, followed by the rest of the team.

"What's going on here?" Clark asked nervously.

"Yeah. I've got a bad feeling about this," Daniels answered.

"Nevertheless, we are out of our current danger. I just hope we can get the power up and running from here," Alyssa said. "Blackwell, Willson, get the med kit and tend to any wounded. The rest of you, find a way to get the power on."

A few minutes later, the power lurched on. The intercom sounded loudly. "*All personnel to the armory, immediately.*"

"You heard him, let's move," Alyssa ordered.

The bridge crew debugged and rebooted the systems.

"Okay. It's time to relearn how to operate these machines," Rimerez said as he pounded on the console keys. "This screen is working."

"External sensors online," Butters reported, echoed by Wallace and Robins as they affirmed communications and internal sensors.

"Great, order the crew to the armory," Jack said as his team returned.

"And scan the station for any non-human life signs," Rimerez added.

"No sign of life except our security team," Wallace replied as he tapped on the console.

"How's it coming with the lights and other systems?"

"Just a few more minutes," Jennings said without looking up.

"Sir, sensors are picking up several ships," Butters reported, he punched a button and instantly the screen on the front wall blinked on, revealing half a dozen ships.

"Mr. Jennings, we need those extra systems up," Jack said urgently. Jennings didn't bother to answer as his fingers flew over the keypad.

"They're docking, sir," Butters reported.

"As soon as you get those systems up, take out those ships," Rimerez told Butters. "Patch me into the intercom."

His voice amplified as he announced to those left on the station:

"This is Rimerez. We've got half a dozen Hamari ships docking, estimations of . . ."

"Twenty-five," reported Butters.

"Twenty-five on each ship."

"I've got it," Jennings shouted as the lights burst into existence.

Bent on the conquest of the space federation, the Hamari stormed through the airlocks and secured the area.

"Clear. No signs of life. We're moving down into the adjoining corridors," reported the commanding officer.

They rounded several corners with no incident, passing a few half-eaten corpses, but no life.

"Signs still show clear, almost to the . . ."

He fell to his knees as he rounded the corner right into the barrel of Jack's firearm. Caught off guard, the Hamari were obliterated.

"Keep moving," Jack ordered as he started down the corridor.

His team didn't make it past the next curve before encountering another onslaught of Hamari. The first shot hit Jack's side, sending him tumbling to the floor. Everything seemed to be happening in slow motion as Porter and Thomas both fell to the floor beside him. His team was being slaughtered.

Jack managed to get to his knees and watched a Hamari soldier train his weapon on him. At that moment, he knew his life was over and strangely he wasn't thinking of dying as he always thought he would. He was remembering Gabriel's words to him. Jack knew that if he were to die, he would spend an eternity in a furnace of fire. He knew he needed to be saved and he knew Christ was the only way. Closing his eyes, knowing they would never again open in this life, he called for Jesus Christ. *Save me, Jesus, I need you . . .*

Suddenly he felt a hand on his shoulder, lifting him to his feet. He opened his eyes and saw his adversary lying dead on the floor. Filled with a new strength, whether from God or himself, he knew not. All he knew was that he was alive and "born again" as Gabriel would have put it. Jack staggered forward, his hand clutching his bleeding side as Officer Thomas secured him and quickly fell back.

Silas and his team retreated into the officers' lounge. "We've got to make our stand here. Jam the doors," he ordered. "We need to set up a perimeter with those chairs and tables."

The crew instantly began overturning the tables and chairs, creating a secure perimeter.

"Okay, as soon as they get through, open fire, but wait until they're in the open to use the grenades. These tables should shield us from most of the blasts."

The officers ducked behind the tables just before the doors exploded into shrapnel, imbedding into the desktops. Instantaneously, the Hamari opened fire blindly. The tabletops splintered as the rounds hit. The officers retaliated with a round of fire of their own. Silas lobbed his grenades over the tables, hoping his fellow officers were following suit. Half a second later, the grenades exploded. Silas pulled a piece of shrapnel from his bloodied shoulder, closed his eyes and prayed for courage and strength as he stood to his feet. He held the trigger down to his weapon, sending an onslaught of ammunition at the entrance doors. The other officers began the same insane maneuver, inspired by Silas's unbelievable act. A few officers received a shot themselves, but kept firing as long as their dying bodies would allow. Silas stepped over the barrier of tables and marched forward. Again, the rest of his soldiers followed him. Within seconds, all but Silas had stopped firing.

"Sir!" Officer Dunlars yelled. "Sir! They are all dead."

He slowly pushed Silas's arms down. Silas scanned the room and peeked out into the hallway.

Alyssa and her team stormed through the second story of the plaza and surrounded the Hamari from above. The first wave of enemy troops had gotten past and forced Jack's team back into the corridors. The second wave, however, stood their ground for a few more minutes, before retreating into the corridor and back into their own docked ships. Alyssa motioned for the officers closest to the spiral stairs to descend while the rest of the officers covered them. Then Alyssa led the rest of the company down.

"Okay. First, we eject those Hamari ships, then we go after the rest. Wilson, Daniels, and Clark, you're with me. The rest of you watch our backs," Alyssa ordered.

A few minutes later, Alyssa's team finished manually ejecting the ships, and they all breathed a sigh of relief. With the stations external weapons now fully operational again, the Hamari ships were destroyed just as soon as they got a safe distance from the station, and the remaining security officers began rounding up the surviving Hamari renegades for trial.

Several days later, the station was back up and running at optimum level, and the Hamari who attempted to take the station had been sent to the highest level maximum security prison colony. Jack, Alyssa, and Silas sat at their table in the balcony of Courtney's Restaurant discussing the events of the past few days.

"All I can think about lately is Gabe," Silas admitted. "How he died, the things he'd said, and how he lived."

"He was a great man," Alyssa replied.

"And a good friend," Silas added. "You know maybe we should look in to the things he's said. You know, about Jesus and all."

"Speaking of that, there's something I've been meaning to tell you guys."

Jack launched into an account of his decision to accept Christ as his Savior during the battle with the Hamari.

Please leave a review on the website where you purchased the book.

Visit C. J. Korryn's website for more of his books.

https://www.cjkorryn.com/books

Connect with C. J. Korryn through:

Website:
https://www.cjkorryn.com

Blog:
https://authorcjkorryn.wixsite.com/blog

Facebook:
https://www.facebook.com/AUTHORCJKORRYN/

Instagram:
https://WWW.instagram.com/cjkorryn/

Serial novel subscription:
https://www.cjkorrynserialsubscriptions.com/

www.ingramcontent.com/pod-product-compliance
Lightning Source LLC
Chambersburg PA
CBHW071358200726
48294CB00004B/1211